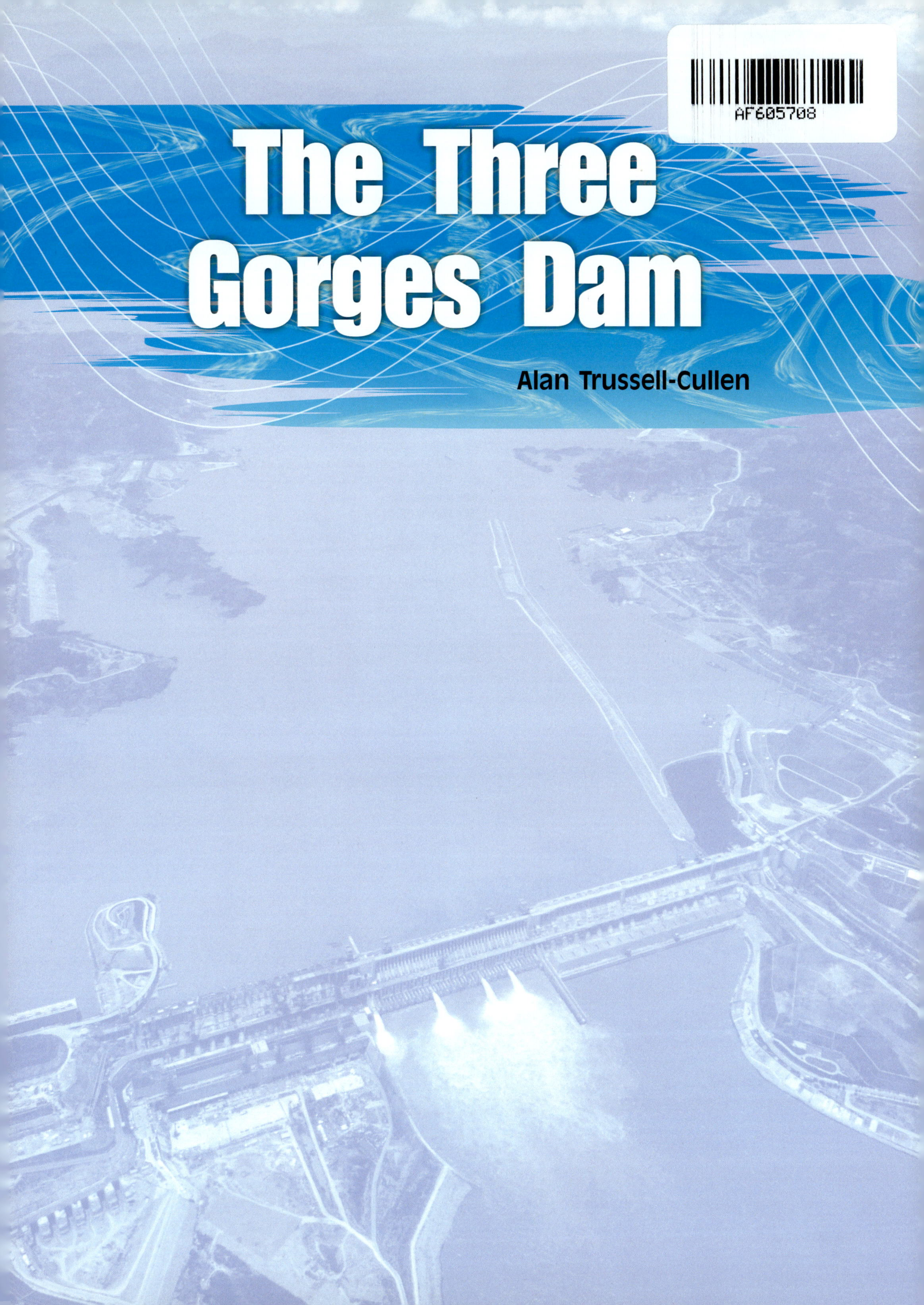

The Three Gorges Dam

Alan Trussell-Cullen

The Three Gorges Dam

Text: Alan Trussell-Cullen
Editor: Vanessa Pellatt
Design: Kerri Wilson
Series design: James Lowe
Photo researcher: Lisa Piemonte
Production controllers: Lisa Porter and Renee Cusmano

Acknowledgements
The author and publisher would like to acknowledge permission to reproduce material from the following sources:
AAP/AFP Photo/Goh Chai Hin: p. 14 (inset); AAP Image/AP Photo: p. 8 (bottom left); AAP Image/AP Photo/Andy Wong: p. 21 (bottom); AAP Image/AP Photo/Ng Han Guan: p. 6 (top left); AAP Image/AP Photo/Vincent Yu: p. 21 (top); Corbis Australia: pp. 1, 3, 6 (bottom & top right), 11 (main), 12 (bottom), 13 (bottom), 23 (top), front and back covers; Getty Images: pp. 8, 9 (top), 10 (both), 12 (top), 14 (main), 16, 20, 23 (bottom); Guy Holt © Cengage Learning Australia: pp. 4–5 (bottom), 11 (inset), 13 (top), 18, 19; Mark Cawardine/ANTPhoto.com.au: p. 17 (bottom); Martin Harvey/ANTPhoto.com.au: p. 17 (top); Mediacolor's: p. 15; Photolibrary: pp. 5, 7, 22; Shutterstock/Albert H. Teich: p. 4.

Every effort has been made to trace and acknowledge copyright. However, if any infringement has occurred, the publishers tender their apologies and invite the copyright holders to contact them.

Fast Forward Independent Texts
Level 16

For product information and technology assistance,
in Australia call 1300 790 853;
in New Zealand call 0508 635 766

For permission to use material from this text or product,
please email **aust.permissions@cengage.com**

ISBN 978 0 17 017999 7
ISBN 978 0 17 017897 6 (set)

Cengage Learning Australia
Level 5, 80 Dorcas Street
Southbank, Victoria Australia 3006

For learning solutions, visit **cengage.com.au**

Printed in Australia by Ligare Pty Ltd
2 3 4 5 6 7 28 27 26 25 24

The Three Gorges Dam

Alan Trussell-Cullen

Contents

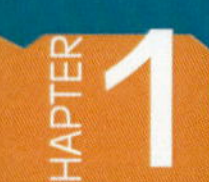

CHAPTER 1

The Three Gorges Dam

The Three **Gorges** Dam is being built on the Yangtze River.

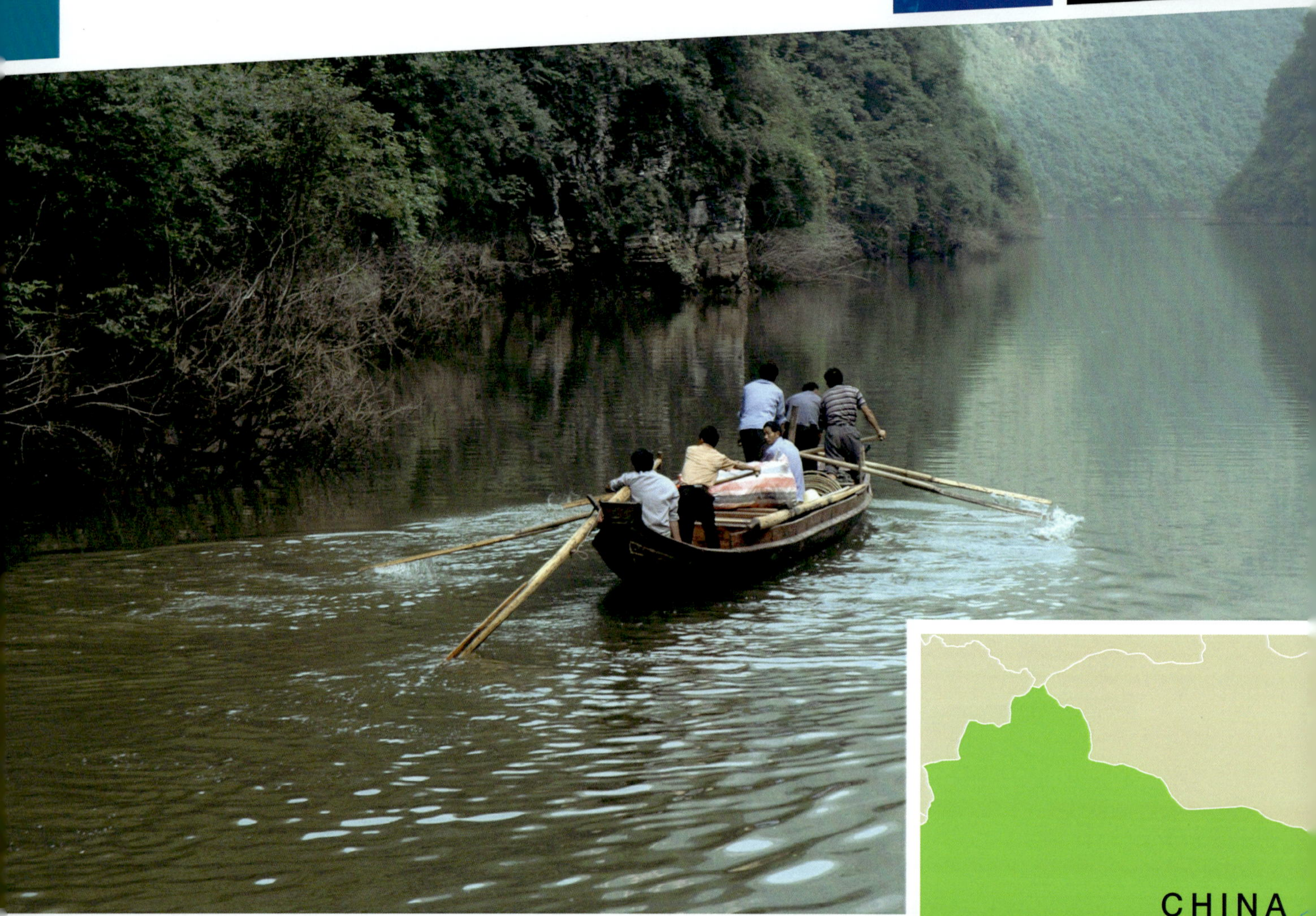

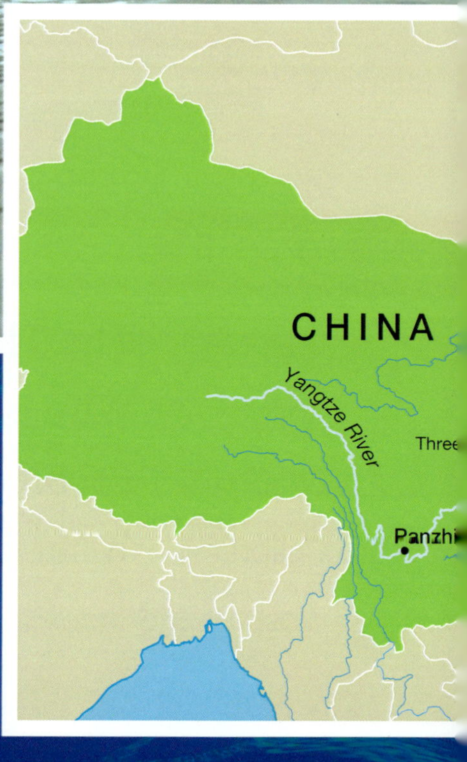

The Yangtze is China's biggest river. It is also the third longest river in the world.

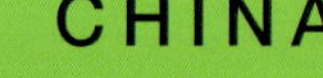

It is called the Three Gorges Dam because it is being built in an area called the Three Gorges.

Even though there is still some work to do on the dam, it is already being used to make power. The water turns **turbines**, making electricity.

building the dam

The force of this water makes energy.

The Three Gorges Dam
is the biggest water-powered
electricity station in the world.

CHAPTER 2

Why Is China Building the Dam?

There are three main reasons why China is building the dam:

- energy
- **flood** control
- transport.

In 1988, the Yangtze River flooded these homes.

Burning coal is polluting this Chinese city.

Energy

Today, most of China's electricity is made by burning coal.

The Three Gorges Dam uses water instead of coal to make electricity. This will cut down on pollution.

This ship carries people and goods along the Yangtze River.

Flood control

A big problem with the Yangtze River is that it floods.
Many people have died or lost their homes in the floods.

The Three Gorges Dam has been built
to help stop these floods.
The dam has flood gates
that will close if the river floods.

When the river rises,
the gates will hold the water
back in the **reservoir**.

Transport

The Yangtze River has always been an important waterway for ships.

In the past,
it was hard for ships
to get through the Three Gorges
because some parts were very **narrow**.
Now, the dam has a **lock**.

ships approaching the lock

The lock helps the ships move up and down the river in stages.

For bigger ships, a ship lift will be built. It will move the ships up and down the river in one stage.

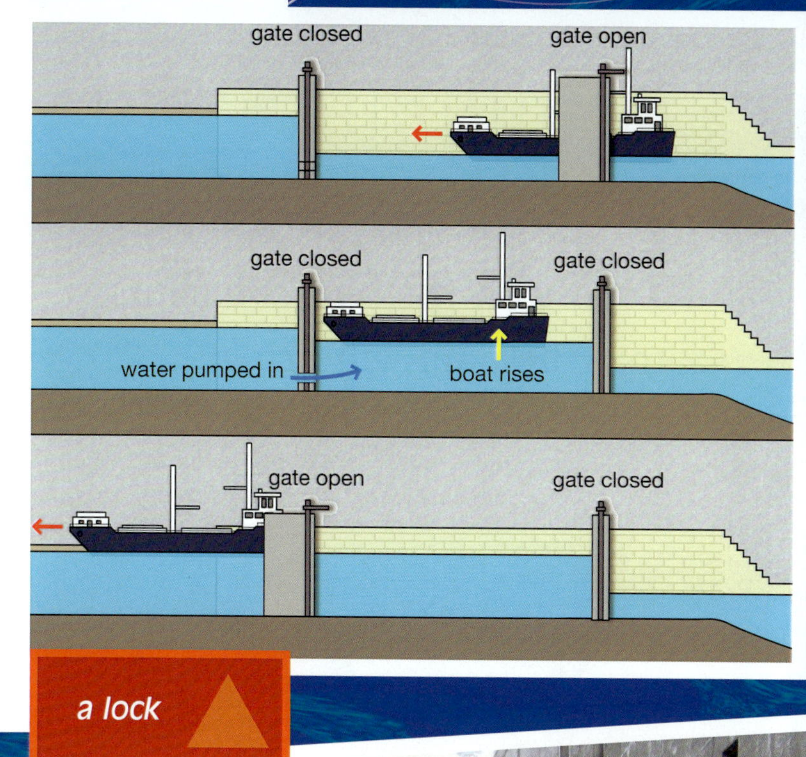

a lock

ships entering the lock

CHAPTER 3

Problems with the Dam

Even with the improvements that the dam will bring, many people in China are unhappy.

Millions of people have been moved to new homes to make way for the dam.

Many people are worried about losing their history and culture.

The Zhang Fei Temple was relocated to make way for the dam.

Some buildings were moved
but other buildings
and important places were lost
when the reservoir filled with water.

Another problem is that the dam makes the river flow more slowly. Pollution then gets trapped in the river.

polluted water in the Yangtze River

The dam will also destroy the **wetlands** around parts of the river. Animals and plants that live in the river and the wetlands will lose their homes.

Large numbers of Siberian Crane spend their winters on the river. There are only about 3000 left in the world and scientists worry that they could become extinct.

The Baiji dolphin is found only in the Yangtze River. It is so rare that scientists believe it is almost extinct.

There is a lot of **silt**
in the Yangtze River.
Silt can cause problems.
It can build up on the bottom
of the dam's reservoir
and fill it up
so the ships get stuck.

silt building up on the bottom of the reservoir

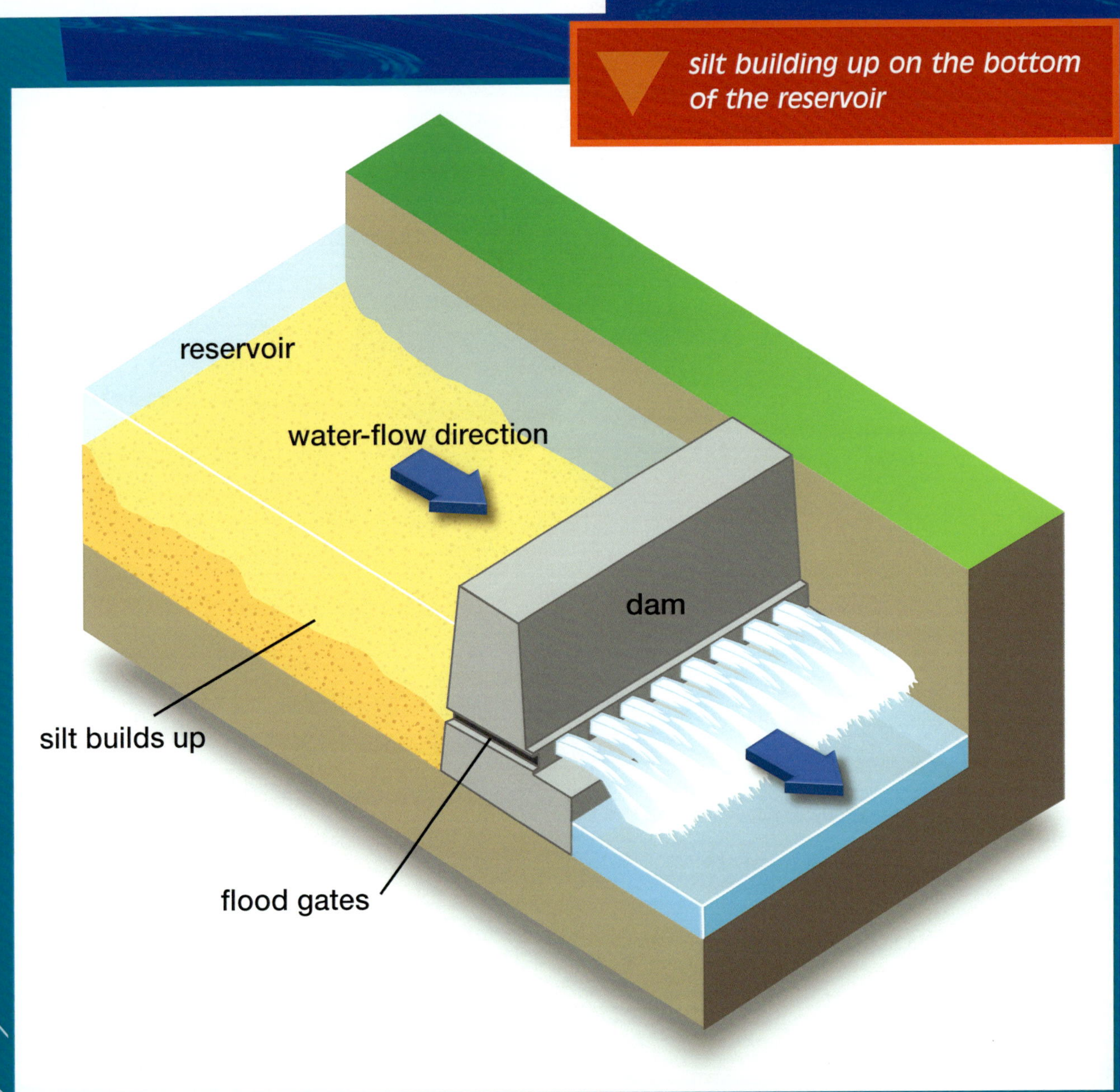

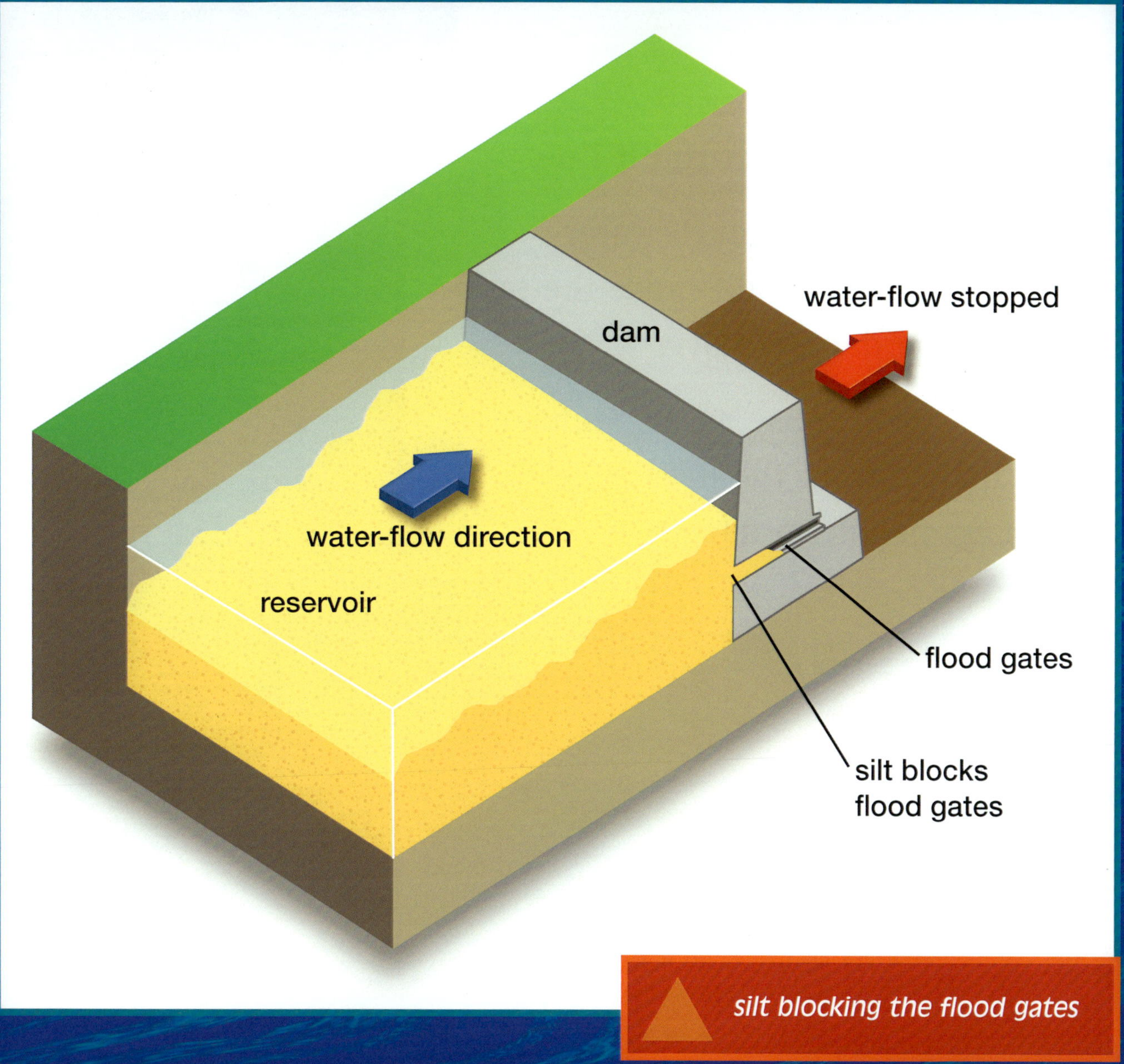

silt blocking the flood gates

Silt could also block the dam's turbines. Then the dam would not be able to make as much electricity.

Or it could stop the dam's flood gates from closing when the river floods.

Some people are worried that the dam sits on a **fault line**.

They fear that too much water in the reservoir could cause the land around the dam to move.

It might even cause an earthquake, which would put the lives of many people in danger.

These cracks were made by an earthquake.

In 2008, earthquakes caused a lot of damage in China.

CHAPTER 4

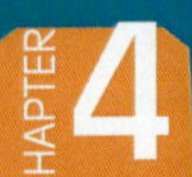

What Does the Future Hold?

There are plans to build more dams
on the Yangtze River
and the rivers
that flow into the Yangtze.

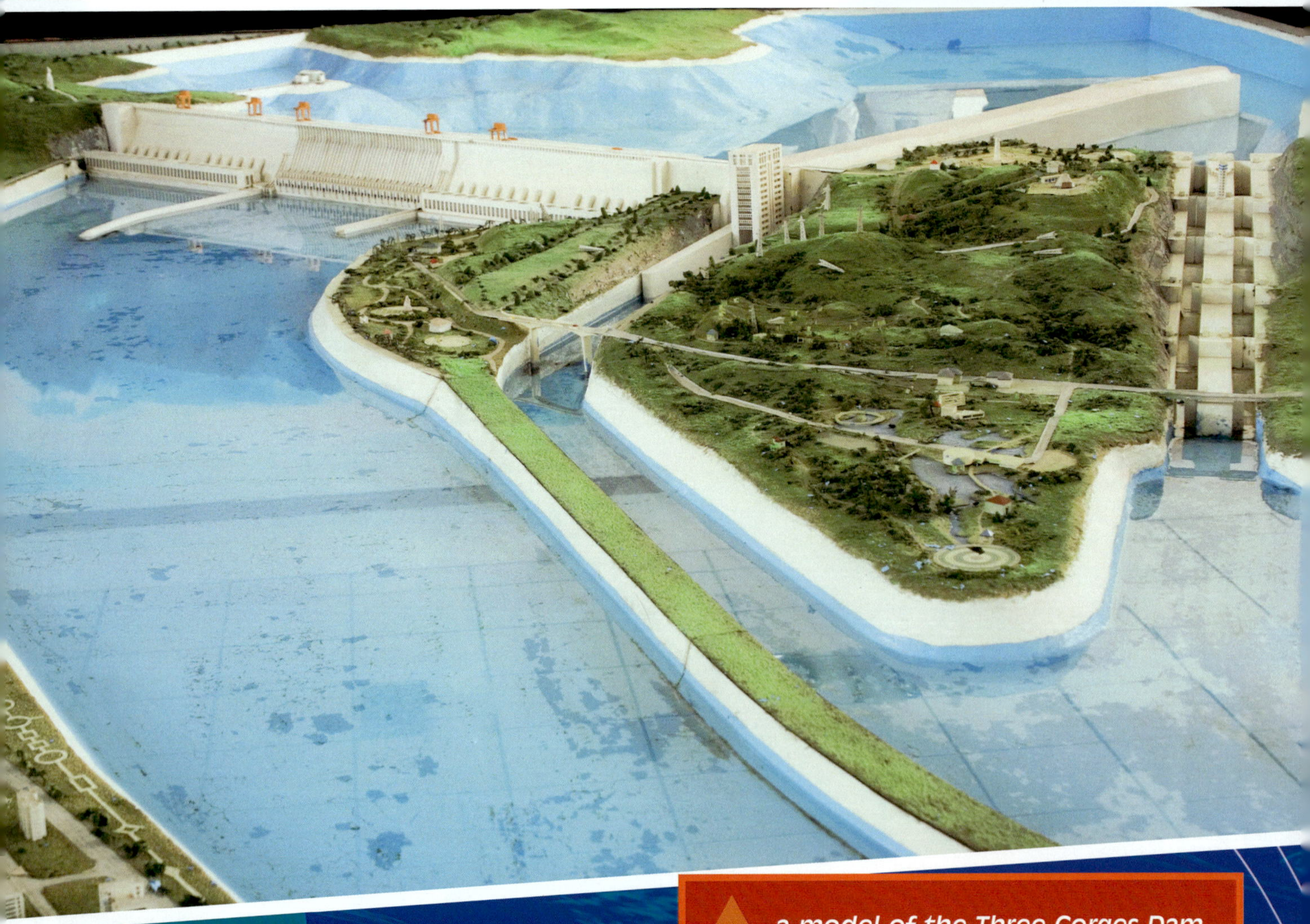

a model of the Three Gorges Dam

This factory in China burns coal.

All these water-powered electricity stations mean that China will not have to use as much coal to make its electricity.

Shanghai, China

Glossary

fault line a crack in Earth's crust

flood when water rises to cover the land

gorges narrow passages between mountains

lock a structure for moving ships up and down a steep part of a river

narrow not wide

reservoir a large natural or artificial lake used for collecting and storing water

silt bits of dirt and sand carried along by the flow of a river

turbine a machine that creates electricity by using the energy that is made by moving water

wetlands land that is often covered in water and is home to lots of animals and plants

Index